Samuel French Acting Edition

Are You Sure?

A Play in Two Acts

by Sam Bobrick

SAMUELFRENCH.COM   SAMUELFRENCH.CO.UK

FOR PRODUCTION ENQUIRIES

UNITED STATES AND CANADA
Info@SamuelFrench.com
1-866-598-8449

UNITED KINGDOM AND EUROPE
Plays@SamuelFrench.co.uk
020-7255-4302

Each title is subject to availability from Samuel French, depending upon country of performance. Please be aware that *ARE YOU SURE?* may not be licensed by Samuel French in your territory. Professional and amateur producers should contact the nearest Samuel French office or licensing partner to verify availability.

MUSIC USE NOTE

Licensees are solely responsible for obtaining formal written permission from copyright owners to use copyrighted music in the performance of this play and are strongly cautioned to do so. If no such permission is obtained by the licensee, then the licensee must use only original music that the licensee owns and controls. Licensees are solely responsible and liable for all music clearances and shall indemnify the copyright owners of the play(s) and their licensing agent, Samuel French, against any costs, expenses, losses and liabilities arising from the use of music by licensees. Please contact the appropriate music licensing authority in your territory for the rights to any incidental music.

IMPORTANT BILLING AND CREDIT REQUIREMENTS

If you have obtained performance rights to this title, please refer to your licensing agreement for important billing and credit requirements.

SYNOPSIS

Are You Sure? is a case of shifting realities. How much is happening, how much isn't? Does David want to kill Caroline? Does Charley want to kill David? Does Caroline want to kill everyone? The play mixes comedy with high suspense as the audience tries to figure out what to believe and who to believe. One thing for sure, someone did it.

Are You Sure? premiered at the Back Alley Theatre, California. It was produced by Laura Zucker and directed by Allan Miller. The cast was as follows:

CAROLINE .... Lois Nettleton

DAVID .... Ronnie Cox

SIMON .... Jack Collins

STEFANIE .... Ellen Maxted

MARIE .... Catherine McLeod

CHARLEY .... Jeffrey Haddow

Set Design: Jim Billings
Lighting: Kraig Aaronson
Costumes: Hilary Sloane
Stage Manager: Michael Wymore

CHARACTERS

CAROLINE

DAVID

MARIE

STEFANIE

SIMON

CHARLEY

TIME & PLACE

Present.

Library of a wealthy home.

ARE YOU SURE?

ACT I

Scene 1

TIME: The present. Evening.

PLACE: An elegantly appointed traditional library in an obviously wealthy home. There is a fireplace and shelves filled with books. The set, built in front of a backdrop, is somewhat illusory. While Stage Center has a realistic core, both ends of the set disappear into a vagueness that allows the actors to enter and exit from the shadows. There are two sets of French doors, one set Stage Right, the other Stage Left. Stage Left at times serves as an exit to the terrace. (The Stage Left doors may be built into the backdrop.)

At Stage Center is a lovely antique sofa which separates two Queen Anne wing back chairs. Behind the sofa is a long, narrow table with room for a wine decanter, whisky decanter, glasses and several books.

CAROLINE OGDEN, a woman in her mid-forties, wearing a very chic lounging gown, sits curled up on the sofa, absorbed in a book. DAVID OGDEN, her husband, a very handsome man approximately Caroline's age, stands in back of one of the chairs with a nearly empty glass of wine, staring pensively at his wife. HE wears a sweater jacket over a shirt and tie.

7

DAVID. I love you. I've never loved anyone as much as I love you. It's a marvelous feeling loving someone as madly, as desperately, as I love you. (*During the following DAVID pours a glass of wine for Caroline, then takes a small vial from his jacket pocket, removes the top carefully and empties the liquid contents slowly into the glass. HE places the cap back on the bottle and returns it to his jacket pocket.*) I know most people still believe I married you for your money, but how wrong I've proven them, haven't I, darling? Of course, I have. (*HE offers the glass of wine to Caroline.*) Wine?

CAROLINE. (*Not looking up.*) No, I don't think so.

DAVID. It might relax you.

CAROLINE. I am relaxed, darling.

DAVID. It might relax you more.

CAROLINE. (*Looking up.*) I don't care for any wine right now, thank you, David.

DAVID. Drink it, Caroline. Do me a favor and drink it. Please.

CAROLINE. You've done something to the wine haven't you? Have you poisoned it again?

DAVID. (*In pain.*) Please drink the wine, Caroline. It'll be the last thing I ask of you. I promise.

CAROLINE. I know you've poisoned it, David. I'm not going to drink it.

DAVID. Why must you make me beg for everything?

CAROLINE. Do I? Perhaps you rather enjoy that. Some people actually do.

DAVID. It's fine wine, Caroline. A Chateau Margaux, '71. You won't be disappointed. I never am.

CAROLINE. Then why don't you drink it, David?

DAVID. You don't think I would?

CAROLINE. No. Your life with me can't be that unbearable.

DAVID. You don't think so? (*DAVID looks at her and then slowly, deliberately drinks down the wine.*) Are you satisfied?

CAROLINE. If you are.

DAVID. (*Laughs haughtily.*) Well, the joke's on you, Caroline. There was nothing in the wine. Nothing.

CAROLINE. Good.

(*DAVID clutches at his throat and stumbles back to his chair and collapses. CAROLINE looks at him for a beat and then continues reading. SIMON ALDEN enters. He is Caroline's father and a man in his mid-sixties.*)

SIMON. Hello, dear.

CAROLINE. Hello, Father.

SIMON. I thought I'd pick out a good book for the night. What are you reading?

CAROLINE. *Jane Eyre.*

SIMON. Again?

CAROLINE. I enjoy it. I know how it begins, I know how it ends. There's not the desperate uncertainty for me anymore. It makes things so much easier.

SIMON. Does it?

CAROLINE. Much easier.

SIMON. Then I'm happy for you. What's wrong with David? Drunk?

CAROLINE. Dead.

SIMON. (*Looks at David.*) My, my.

CAROLINE. He poisoned my wine and in the end drank it himself.

SIMON. I do hope you're not going to be too upset by this.

CAROLINE. I don't think I will be. As a matter of fact, I'm handling it much better than the last time, don't you think?

SIMON. Yes. Yes, you are. Much better. (*Takes a book.*) I think I'll try *Moby Dick* again. I love looking for the message. Good night, dear.

CAROLINE. Goodnight, Father.

(*HE exits. CAROLINE reads for a few more beats, then looks over at David sighs, puts her book down and calls to him.*)

CAROLINE. David! David! (*SHE goes to him and shakes him.*) David, you've fallen asleep again.

DAVID. Huh?

CAROLINE. You drink too much, you know that?

DAVID. I suppose so. But one has to have some pleasure in life.

CAROLINE. I've always thought you had too many pleasures.

DAVID. (*Pouring more wine into his glass.*) Have you? Well, we're all entitled to our opinions. Finished your book?

CAROLINE. No, not yet.

DAVID. *Jane Eyre* again, I suppose.

CAROLINE. You know it is.

DAVID. Still find it safe?

CAROLINE. Yes. Threatening at times but in the end, quite safe.

DAVID. They're dead, you know.

CAROLINE. Who?

DAVID. All the people in the book.

CAROLINE. Don't be silly, the main characters survive and live happily ever after.

DAVID. Nonsense. The book was written well over a hundred years ago. Even those who survive the story would now be considered dead for all practical purposes.

CAROLINE. I really don't care to think about it.

DAVID. But you should. It's part of life. Aging, death, funerals ... strokes, paralysis ...

CAROLINE. You try so hard to ruin everything for me, David.

DAVID. I love you. I'm concerned. I don't want you to be hurt.

CAROLINE. How could I possibly be hurt reading *Jane Eyre*, a story about a woman who, despite a miserable beginning, finds happiness.

DAVID. Have you considered that years after the happy ending she probably died childless, alone, a wretched, wrinkled, ugly old hag, toothless and sagging.

CAROLINE. You're really miserable with me, aren't you?

DAVID. I didn't think you noticed.

CAROLINE. And you never thought that possible.

DAVID. Never.

CAROLINE. I did.

DAVID. Good. Then you're not disappointed.

CAROLINE. In you? No, my life with you has lived up to my highest expectations.

DAVID. Then, my darling, you got your money's worth.

CAROLINE. Why does it always come back to money, David?

DAVID. It's possible that's all we have left.

CAROLINE. I'm going to bed. Are you coming?

DAVID. Later.

CAROLINE. Of course. You'd rather wait here for Marie, right?

DAVID. I've never understood hate with jealousy. I would assume that hate could stand quite nicely by itself.

CAROLINE. It can, David. It does. I'm not blind. I see the way you look at each other, you and the maid, David. An ordinary housemaid. Not to mention the vast age difference. It's disgusting.

DAVID. Is this really what you think?

CAROLINE. This is what I know.

DAVID. Is it? Well, then, the fact that I prefer her to you should reveal something, shouldn't it, Caroline? What is it she has that you lack? Could it be warmth, affection, respect ...

CAROLINE. If you find her so marvelous, why don't you leave me and run off with her?

DAVID. Perhaps one day I will.

CAROLINE. You never will. You're far too weak.

DAVID. I'm much stronger that the others.

CAROLINE. You're wrong. The others weren't as weak as you,

DAVID.. Not even Charley. Charley used you.

CAROLINE. Charley loved me.

DAVID. Where is he? If he loved you so much, where is he?

CAROLINE. (*Stunned.*) I ... I don't know.

DAVID. Good night, Caroline

CAROLINE. (*SHE holds him. HE remains aloof.*) What if I promised to change? To be warm and loving and tender?

DAVID. But for what reason?

CAROLINE. To start all over.

DAVID. (*HE frees himself from her hold.*) No, I'm sorry. That can't happen.

CAROLINE. (*Pursuing him.*) Touch me, David. I want you to touch me.

DAVID. (*Backing away.*) No ... No, I can't.

CAROLINE. (*Turning her back to him.*) Massage my neck, David. I know it will make me feel better.

DAVID. No. No.

CAROLINE. Put your hands on my neck, David. They're so warm. It relieves me so.

DAVID. (*Starts to massage her neck.*) No, I don't want to.

CAROLINE. Oh, that's nice. So nice.

DAVID. (*His hands start to clutch her throat.*) I can't stand to touch you. You know that.

CAROLINE. You always used to touch me. You used to love to touch me and hold me.

DAVID. No! No, I never did. (*Pulls his hands away from her; calling.*) Marie! Where is Marie?

CAROLINE. A maid, David. Why must you degrade yourself with a maid?

DAVID. Maybe you'd like to watch us make love. Maybe you'd like to see what you were capable of once. (*Calls again.*) Marie! Marie!

CAROLINE. I'm going to put a stop to this. I'm going to!

(CAROLINE picks up the letter opener lying on the table and plunges it into David's back. DAVID moans, staggers a little and falls to the floor.
STEFANIE, a beautiful girl in her early twenties, enters. She is dressed as a maid. SHE looks at David. SHE watches him gasp and fall to his chair. SHE sees the letter opener in Caroline's hand. SHE screams.)

STEFANIE. Oh, my God, Mrs. Ogden. You've done it!

CAROLINE. No, no, Marie. It's nothing. You'll see, it's nothing.

STEFANIE. He's dead. He said you would do this. He said you would.

CAROLINE. No. No, Marie. He lied to you. That's what he wanted you to believe. Besides, it's nothing, Marie. It's always nothing. You'll see.

STEFANIE. You're a murderer! Murderer! *(STEFANIE runs off in horror.)*

CAROLINE. *(Some doubt now.)* It's always nothing. *(CAROLINE lays the letter opener down, goes to David and apprehensively shakes him.)* David! David!

DAVID. Huh, oh.

CAROLINE. *(Relieved.)* See, I haven't done it. I knew I didn't do it.

DAVID. What?

CAROLINE. Kill you!

DAVID. Again?

CAROLINE. We had a terrible quarrel, and I plunged the letter opener into your back.

DAVID. Oh, my.

CAROLINE. Is that all? Is that your only response to your possible death?

DAVID. (*Filled with love and compassion for Caroline.*) But I'm not dead and you haven't done it.

CAROLINE. That's true. But it seems to be more realistic each time. This time I felt the blood on my hands, David. Look, it's not on them but I feel it. So real ... so wet. (*SHE holds up her hand. There is no blood on it.*)

DAVID. I'll bet you've forgotten to take your medicine. Haven't you?

CAROLINE. No, Marie hasn't brought it yet.

DAVID. Not yet? That's strange. (*Calling.*) Marie!

CAROLINE. It was so real. Each time it gets more real.

DAVID. You mustn't forget to take your medicine, darling.

CAROLINE. I'm sorry, David. It's not my fault.

DAVID. Of course not, sweetheart.

CAROLINE. You ... You're not angry?

DAVID. How can I be angry with you? You're just going through some bad times. I adore you.

CAROLINE. Yes, you do ... or so you tell me.

(*DAVID looks at her for beat. MARIE, a uniformed maid in her mid-sixties enters.*)

MARIE. Yes?

DAVID. Marie, you forgot Mrs. Ogden's medicine.

MARIE. No, sir. I brought it to her right before ten, when she always takes it.

CAROLINE. (*Looking at Marie curiously.*) You did?

MARIE. Yes.

CAROLINE. You're Marie?

DAVID. (*Soothing.*) Caroline.

CAROLINE. She's much older than before, isn't she?

DAVID. No, dear. Marie's been that age as long as I can remember.

MARIE. I did bring you your medicine, Mrs. Ogden. Mr. Ogden was asleep right there in the chair. You were reading.

CAROLINE. Did you?

MARIE. Yes. Of course.

CAROLINE. You'd like me to believe that, wouldn't you?

MARIE. No, ma'am. I did.

CAROLINE. Who are you, Marie? Who are you?

MARIE. Please, Mrs. Ogden.

DAVID. Easy, dear. You don't want to have another of your spells. You don't want to go through that again.

CAROLINE. (*A bit giddy.*) A spell? I've never had a spell, David. A hallucination, possibly, but something as outdated as a spell ... People don't use those terms any more. A seizure, even that's more current.

DAVID. If you like, Marie can give you a shot.

CAROLINE. A shot? Why not? Dope her up so that she can't see what's going on. Cloud her mind so that she can't tell reality from illusion. And afterwards the two of you can come down here and make love. He'll make love to you on that sofa, Marie, like he should make love to me.

MARIE. It breaks my heart to see her like this.

CAROLINE. You're doing this to me, David. I know you're doing this to me.

DAVID. You'd better bring another pill, Marie.

MARIE. Right away, sir. (*MARIE starts out.*)

CAROLINE. No, don't go. Don't go. I don't want to be left alone with him.

MARIE. (*Looks at her pathetically.*) He loves you, Mrs. Ogden. (*SHE exits.*)

CAROLINE. I don't want to be alone ... wretched ... wrinkled ... alone.

DAVID. (*Menacing.*) You don't have to, Caroline. There are ways to avoid all that. Simple ways. You do understand what I'm talking about, don't you, Caroline?

CAROLINE. I know what you're doing, David. I know and in the end, I'll beat you. You'll see. I will. I will.

DAVID. (*Picks up Caroline's book and looks at it.*) Edgar Allan Poe. I didn't think you liked tales of the macabre.

(*STEFANIE enters as Marie.*)

STEFANIE. Mrs. Ogden. Your pill.

DAVID. Oh, thank you, Marie. Take your pill, Caroline.

CAROLINE. (*Confused.*) I ...

DAVID. Please take your pill, darling, and everything will be better. I promise.

CAROLINE. But I ... I ... thought ...

DAVID. Caroline, dear Caroline. You're my whole world. The sun that warms me, the moon that poets write about. Please take the pill.

(*CAROLINE takes the glass of water and the pill. STEFANIE goes to David and puts her arms around him.*)

STEFANIE. We've got to finish it soon, David.
DAVID. We will.
STEFANIE. Now, David, now. What if she catches on? (*Kisses him.*)
DAVID. We will finish it soon.

(THEY kiss. CAROLINE watches them. THEY turn to her innocently.)

CAROLINE. I've taken the pill, David. I really think I do feel much better. Are you pleased?

(The stage dims slowly.)

End of Scene 1

Scene 2

The next day. Late morning.
The library.
SIMON is in the library, waiting. HE is wearing a suit. DAVID enters through the French doors with three books which HE places around the room.

DAVID. Hello, Simon. To what do I owe the pleasure?
SIMON. I've got to talk to you about Caroline.
DAVID. Really? Frankly, at this point, I find Caroline's life none of your business.
SIMON. David, I don't like what's happening.
DAVID. I'm sorry but there's nothing I can do about it.

SIMON. I don't believe that for a moment.

DAVID. She's spoken to you, hasn't she? Well, whatever she's told you is not the way things are.

SIMON. Then you tell me the way things are and let me decide for myself.

DAVID. You still love her, don't you? (*HE pours himself a glass of wine.*)

SIMON. I never denied that.

DAVID. Let go, Simon. You're in love with someone who doesn't exist anymore. Yesterday's shadow, yesterday's dream. She doesn't even faintly resemble the Caroline you married, a marriage, by the way, we both knew was doomed from the start.

SIMON. That never mattered. What mattered was having Caroline. She was something then. Young, vibrant, in love with life, everything your boyhood fantasies told you a woman was supposed to be.

DAVID. That was years ago.

SIMON. (*Recalling.*) She was only eighteen when we met. She was going through analysis, into father figures. The timing for me was perfect. Sure, I was shattered when it was over, but I had those wonderful years. I relish every minute I had with her. Just the same way I hate every minute I spend away from her.

DAVID. You're a lucky man, Simon. You can live with the memories. I live with the reality, and I don't know how much longer I can take it.

SIMON. *You are* in pain, aren't you?

DAVID. Pain is too kind a word.

SIMON. What I would give to feel that pain.

DAVID. And what I would do to be rid of it.

(THEY look at each other for a beat. MARIE enters.)

MARIE. Excuse me, Mr. Ogden. You have a call in the living room.
DAVID. Do you mind, Simon?
SIMON. I have nothing but time.
DAVID. Thank you, Marie.

(DAVID exits. MARIE stays behind.)

SIMON. Marie.
MARIE. Mr. Curtis.
SIMON. You're looking splendid, Marie.
MARIE. Thank you.
SIMON. I'm surprised. I never would have guessed you'd still be here.
MARIE. Some of us have an ability to hang on.
SIMON. That's an art in itself, isn't it?
MARIE. Besides, there's a great need for me now.
SIMON. Really?
MARIE. Yes. I find I'm much more useful than I've ever been and it is important to be useful.
SIMON. No matter what the purpose?
MARIE. *(A pensive beat.)* Excuse me. I must see to lunch. *(SHE starts out.)*
SIMON. Marie! *(MARIE stops and turns to him.)* In a way, I'm happy for you.

(MARIE looks at him for a beat, turns and exits. SIMON sighs and picks up a book on a nearby table and leafs through it. STEFANIE enters through the French doors.

SHE is now wearing a casual but revealing ensemble and carries a croquet mallet.)

STEFANIE. *(Calling.)* David! *(SHE sees Simon.)* Oh, I'm sorry. *(SHE starts out.)*

SIMON. Don't go. I love to look at a pretty face.

STEFANIE. How sweet.

SIMON. David is on the phone in the other room. I'm Simon Curtis, Caroline's first husband.

STEFANIE. I'm Stefanie, David's private secretary.

SIMON. David has a secretary? For what?

STEFANIE. I'm typing his new book.

SIMON. New book? I didn't know he had an old book. I didn't even know he was a writer.

STEFANIE. Well, he's not yet. But soon he'll write something and then he will be.

SIMON. And how long has this been going on?

STEFANIE. Monday will make it two months.

SIMON. It's a nice job.

STEFANIE. Yes, but not without its insecurities.

SIMON. Such as?

STEFANIE. I can't type.

SIMON. I have a hunch that isn't important. May I be candid?

STEFANIE. If you must.

SIMON. What does she think?

STEFANIE. Caroline? She's thrilled.

SIMON. Really?

STEFANIE. Oh, don't be an old fool. Of course, she feels terrible. She's hurt, she's worried, she's frightened of every minute he's with me. But those are the breaks of the game, aren't they? She's had her turn ...

SIMON. And now it's yours.

STEFANIE. Exactly. The old make way for the new.

SIMON. Seems to me I've heard that story before.

STEFANIE. Have you?

SIMON. Yes, and unfortunately they were speaking of me.

STEFANIE. (*Smiles*.) I've never met her second husband. Charley! I like that name. He was younger than she, wasn't he? Twelve years younger, I heard. Was it a scandal? It must have been.

SIMON. A scandal? Why does yesterday always seem so damn Victorian to the young? That liaison was more of a curiosity but Caroline found it exciting. She was different then. Free, uncomplicated, no conscience what-so-ever.

STEFANIE. I'm like that, you know.

SIMON. Yes, I think so.

STEFANIE. Free as the wind. Nothing to stop me; nothing to worry me. A basic toy. So simple. So fresh. So provocative. I don't mean to brag. It just happens to be a fact.

SIMON. I accept that.

STEFANIE. These are my days now, and I intend to make the most of them.

SIMON. Youth can be so cruel.

STEFANIE. Only when you don't have it.

SIMON. If David leaves her, he loses everything.

STEFANIE. We know that. It would be absurd to give up all this. But there are other ways. Other ways are sometimes the best ways.

SIMON. It's murder you're talking about, isn't it?

STEFANIE. I hope I wasn't that specific.

SIMON. It'll never happen.

STEFANIE. You don't know that.

SIMON. He's not strong enough.

STEFANIE. No? Would you like to kiss me?

SIMON. More than anything.

STEFANIE. Go ahead.

SIMON. Really? May I? I won't seem foolish or dissipated?

(STEFANIE kisses him. DAVID enters during the kiss and looks at them.)

STEFANIE. Memories?

SIMON. Yes.

STEFANIE. Painful ones?

SIMON. Very.

STEFANIE. Do you really think he's not strong enough?

SIMON. I don't know now.

DAVID. Do you like her, Simon?

SIMON. Yes.

DAVID. She's a lot like Caroline was, isn't she?

SIMON. Yes.

DAVID. I have to do something drastic, Simon.

SIMON. Why bother to tell me?

DAVID. Maybe I would enjoy the approval.

SIMON. I loved her. How I loved her.

DAVID. And what did it get you?

SIMON. That's the difference between us, David. I wasn't out to get anything.

DAVID. Well I'm out to get even.

SIMON. You haven't a chance.

DAVID. You're wrong.

STEFANIE. He says you're not strong enough.

DAVID. I will be when the time comes.

SIMON. Ha!

DAVID. She's not going to have it her way forever. You'll see.

STEFANIE. Good for you, David. (*SHE goes to him.*)

CAROLINE. (*Enters room carrying a croquet mallet.*) David?

DAVID. Yes.

CAROLINE. Who were you talking to?

DAVID. No one, dear.

CAROLINE. I heard you talking to someone.

DAVID. No, no one, dear.

CAROLINE. (*Curious.*) Are you all right?

DAVID. Yes, of course.

CAROLINE. (*Goes to French windows.*) It's a lovely day. I'd like to play some croquet.

DAVID. You know I despise croquet, Caroline.

CAROLINE. Well, I want to play, David, and if I want to play, then we shall play.

DAVID. Caroline, I'm important to you. I really am. People who know us have told me how much better off you are now that I'm here to watch over you.

CAROLINE. You look troubled, David. Is something wrong?

DAVID. No. Nothing.

CAROLINE. That's good. I wouldn't want anything to trouble you. My sweet, wonderful David. How lucky you are to be you.

DAVID. Yes.

CAROLINE. And we're such good friends, aren't we? We're such very good, good friends.

DAVID. I've tried to be.

CAROLINE. Yes, you have. You're not like the others. You would never do anything but be kind and thoughtful. Did you notice I didn't say grateful, David? I promised I wouldn't say it any more. I didn't say it. Coming David?

DAVID. Yes ... coming.

(CAROLINE goes off. DAVID turns to Simon.)

DAVID. You see why I must stop this? You see why I must find a way to stop this? (*HE takes Stefanie's croquet mallet and exits.*)

SIMON. I don't feel sorry for him. Not in the least bit. He's a weak fool.

STEFANIE. Weak? Yes. But unfortunately he's no fool which makes the situation even more difficult. Would you like to kiss me again?

End of Scene 2

Scene 3

Another day. Afternoon
The library.
CHARLEY BRADSHAW, a good-looking man in his mid-thirties, paces nervously in the library. HE is wearing a sports jacket and is tieless. MARIE enters.

MARIE. (*Coldly.*) Mrs. Ogden will be right down. May I get something for you while you're waiting?

CHARLEY. A new life. How's that, Marie?

MARIE. It's a little too late for that, I'm happy to say.

CHARLEY. I see you still possess that winning personality.

MARIE. Along with a very good memory.

CHARLEY. That's too bad. There are certain things everyone should forget.

MARIE. Some people have that ability. Some people don't.

CHARLEY. And some people are a pain in the ass.

MARIE. And some people have no damn class. (*SHE starts out.*)

CHARLEY. You know, Marie, at times I find you very hard to like.

(MARIE exits.)

CHARLEY. (*To himself, aloud.*) But then that's my problem, isn't it.

(CHARLEY lights a cigarette and then looks out the French doors. CAROLINE enters. SHE seems very much in control of herself. CAROLINE looks at Charley for a few beats. His back is to her and HE does not see her.)

CAROLINE. Hello, Charley.

CHARLEY. Hello, Caroline. I assume you're looking well.

CAROLINE. Are you afraid to look?

CHARLEY. (*Turns to her.*) Hello, Caroline. You're looking well.

CAROLINE. Caroline, you look ravishing. I would have liked that. Caroline, you look more beautiful now than when we were married. I would have liked that, too. Caroline, you look like a piece of crap. I think I would have even liked that. At least I would have known what you're really thinking. But Caroline, you're looking well. You could describe a house plant that way, couldn't you?

CHARLEY. (*A beat.*) Yes.

CAROLINE. (*Sighs.*) What kind of trouble are you in now?

CHARLEY. Just trouble. Isn't that enough?

CAROLINE. The last time it cost me thirty thousand.

CHARLEY. This time I need more. This time I need ... fifty.

CAROLINE. Fifty?

CHARLEY. I must have it. I must.

CAROLINE. No. No more, Charley.

CHARLEY. Fifty is nothing to you.

CAROLINE. When I made the ten thousands too easy, you asked for twenty. When I made the twenties too easy, you asked for thirty. You've progressed Charley. You're jumping right into fifty.

CHARLEY. It's nothing to you.

CAROLINE. No.

CHARLEY. You always start off saying "no," but you give it to me anyway.

CAROLINE. This time I mean it. No.

CHARLEY. They'll come after me.

CAROLINE. No, Charley. No more.

CHARLEY. They came after me once. You saw what they did to me.

CAROLINE. No more money, Charley. I won't be used anymore.

CHARLEY. I wouldn't ask if I weren't so desperate. You know that I need the money. It means nothing to you.

CAROLINE. No, Charley.

CHARLEY. You'll never see me again. Is that what you want?

CAROLINE. Yes.

CHARLEY. (*Grabs her.*) Look at me. Is that what you want?

CAROLINE. I don't know. I don't know.

CHARLEY. I'm warning you, Caroline.

CAROLINE. Hold me, Charley.

CHARLEY. The money first, Caroline.

CAROLINE. Will you hold me then?

CHARLEY. A check, Caroline.

(CAROLINE goes to the desk drawer, removes a checkbook and writes a check.)

CHARLEY. I knew you'd come through for me, Caroline.

CAROLINE. (*Dangling the check in front of him.*) Hold me now, Charley.

CHARLEY. (*Takes Caroline in his arms for a beat, then pulls the check from her and starts off.*) Thank you, Caroline.

CAROLINE. You promised.

CHARLEY. I always promise. I'll see you, Caroline.

CAROLINE. Why do you do this to me, Charley?

CHARLEY. You know very well why.

CAROLINE. I won't let you do it again, Charley. I'll be stronger next time.

CHARLEY. Don't fool yourself, Caroline.

CAROLINE. Where are you going?

CHARLEY. Where do you think?

CAROLINE. Back to your women. Who is it this time? Joanne? Suzy? Margo?

CHARLEY. I loved them. I don't love you.

CAROLINE. But you always come back to me. You come back to me when you're in trouble. You'll come back.

CHARLEY. Yes, I will. When I need you. Only when I need you. (*HE leaves through the French door.*)

CAROLINE. (*Calls out to him.*) I did something bad to you, Charley, didn't I? What was it? Tell me. You've got to tell me this time.

(*There is no answer. CHARLEY is gone. DAVID enters. HE is in a suit and tie and carries an attaché case.*)

DAVID. I'm going, Caroline.

CAROLINE. (*Upset.*) He was here again, David. He just left. I swear. Look, see. I gave him another check. It was for fifty thousand dollars this time. I gave it to him. I swear.

DAVID. (*Disappointed.*) Caroline, let's not go into this again.

CAROLINE. He *was* here, David. This time he was really here. (*Shows him checkbook.*) Do you want to see my checkbook?

DAVID. (*Ignores checkbook.*) I should be back in a couple of days.

CAROLINE. You don't care.

DAVID. Of course, I care but what can I do about it? If it gets too difficult, take the pills, all right?

CAROLINE. (*Composing herself.*) Yes.

DAVID. You always feel better after the pills.

CAROLINE. Yes.

DAVID. Good-bye.

CAROLINE. Wait, David. Please kiss me good-bye.

DAVID. All right.

(DAVID kisses her. THEY embrace.)

CAROLINE. That was good, David. That's the way it should be all the time, don't you think so? See, I *can* be warm and wonderful. And I'll bet I can laugh and make jokes and throw wonderful lavish parties again with everyone looking at me, admiring me, envying me.

DAVID. I've got to go, Caroline.

CAROLINE. Why can't it be like this all the time?

DAVID. I don't know.

CAROLINE. Yes, you do. You know perfectly well why.

DAVID. You're blaming me.

CAROLINE. No, I mean I'm trying not to.

DAVID. (*Angry.*) It seems to me you're not trying hard enough. (*HE breaks away from her.*)

CAROLINE. (*Desperate.*) No, no. Don't get angry. Charley gets angry. I can't bear it when you get angry too.

DAVID. Charley is dead, Caroline. Charley's been dead for eight years.

CAROLINE. He isn't.

DAVID. I don't know what to do anymore, Caroline. I can't even seem to conjure up sympathy.

CAROLINE. He was here. No ... No, I mean ... He isn't dead.

DAVID. Then he isn't. Okay? Does that make you feel better? He isn't dead. He's alive. And there's nothing wrong. And the world is filled with sunshine. And you're a happy woman, Caroline. A very happy, glowing, fulfilled, satisfied woman again.

CAROLINE. Yes, yes, that would be nice. That would be very nice. That's the way I really want it to be, and who knows, maybe that's the way it is.

(SHE looks out the French doors. STEFANIE enters. She is wearing an elegant yet provocative dress.)

STEFANIE. Mother?

CAROLINE. Mother?

STEFANIE. I'll drive David to the train, okay?

CAROLINE. I don't want to be left alone.

STEFANIE. Marie is here. Grandfather is here.

CAROLINE. *(Turns and looks at her.)* You're so young, so beautiful. I was like you once. I was exactly like you.

DAVID. Here we go again.

STEFANIE. Come on, David. You don't want to miss your train.

CAROLINE. It wasn't that long ago. My hair would hang down to my shoulders. And I would sit naked in front of a mirror and brush it. I'd brush it for hours.

STEFANIE. You told me this before, Mother.

CAROLINE. I did?

STEFANIE. Come on, David. (*SHE starts out.*)

CAROLINE. Wait. Tell me. Did you know Charley?

STEFANIE. Of course, I knew him, Mother.

CAROLINE. Did you know he's dead?

STEFANIE. Yes, I know he's dead.

CAROLINE. Is he really? How?

STEFANIE. How what?

CAROLINE. How did he die?

DAVID. Why do you do this to yourself, Caroline?

CAROLINE. How did he die?

STEFANIE. I ... I don't know.

CAROLINE. Then maybe he isn't dead.

STEFANIE. He is, Mother, He is. You know he is.

CAROLINE. David, come here.

DAVID. Caroline, I ...

CAROLINE. You're leaving, David. Kiss me good-bye.

DAVID. (*Looks helplessly at Stefanie.*) I did, Caroline.

CAROLINE. Kiss me again. In front of her.

STEFANIE. Mother.

CAROLINE. I want you to, David. I demand it.

STEFANIE. (*Going to her.*) Mother.

CAROLINE. You love him, don't you? Admit it, you love him. You'd like nothing better than to take him from me.

DAVID. For God's sake, Caroline.

CAROLINE. (*To Stefanie.*) You've slept with him, haven't you?

STEFANIE. (*Screaming.*) Stop it, Mother! Stop it!

CAROLINE. You hate me, don't you? Both of you. Sometimes I think I know why, and sometimes I don't ... I'll drive you to the train David.

DAVID. No!

CAROLINE. You're my husband, David. What do you see in this little tramp?

DAVID. All the things that you lack, Caroline. Warmth, kindness, compassion, admiration ...

CAROLINE. She admires you? Hah! Lucky for her they haven't made poor judgement a federal crime.

STEFANIE. *(Turns to David, determined.)* I have to leave here, David.

DAVID. Are you sure you want to?

STEFANIE. More than anything.

CAROLINE. No, please, don't. You can't.

STEFANIE. Why not? I love David and he loves me. I can't stay here any more. Surely you can see that?

CAROLINE. I won't have anyone then. And now Charley's dead, Charley's dead.

STEFANIE. How long do you think a man can love a mad woman, Mother?

CAROLINE. This isn't happening. This really isn't happening.

STEFANIE. Take me in your arms, David. I love you.

DAVID. And I love you.

CAROLINE. I've got to stop this.

(STEFANIE and DAVID embrace and kiss. CAROLINE picks up a letter opener.)

CAROLINE. This will change things. I know it will. It always has.

(CAROLINE plunges the letter opener into Stefanie's back. STEFANIE screams and drops to the floor.)

DAVID. (*Matter-of-fact.*) Not the letter opener again.

CAROLINE. (*Calmed down.*) I had to stop it. It always worked before. (*SHE drops the letter opener near Stefanie's body.*)

DAVID. I know.

CAROLINE. This time I was certain it was the real thing.

DAVID. But it wasn't.

CAROLINE. No, I'm quite sure.

DAVID. Good.

CAROLINE. I mean I'm fairly sure it wasn't ... Was she really my daughter, David?

DAVID. Couldn't you tell?

CAROLINE. Well, yes ... No. Not really. I know I like to have had a daughter ... someone.

DAVID. You could have been a wonderful mother.

CAROLINE. It may have changed everything.

DAVID. Perhaps.

CAROLINE. Yes. (*A beat.*) She's still lying there, David.

DAVID. She'll be gone soon.

CAROLINE. I hope so. Sometimes it's so frightening.

DAVID. (*Looking at the body.*) She is beautiful, isn't she?

CAROLINE. What if I shook her, David? That might do it.

DAVID. I've got a train to catch, Caroline.

CAROLINE. (*Shaking Stefanie.*) Stefanie, you've got to take David to his train. Stefanie. Stefanie, you'll be so disappointed if he leaves without you.

DAVID. Caroline, I've really got to go. You try to handle this one by yourself.

CAROLINE. She won't move, David. Are you sure everything will be right again, are you?

DAVID. (*Picks up book on table.*) *Crime and Punishment.* I liked it all but the ending.

(*DAVID exits. CAROLINE continues to try to arouse Stefanie.*)

CAROLINE. Come on, Stefanie. There's nothing wrong. You know I wouldn't hurt you.

MARIE. (*Enters.*) Mrs. Ogden. Your husband called from the airport. His plane came in early and he's on his way home. (*Notices the body.*) Mrs. Ogden. Oh, my God, Mrs. Ogden. What have you done?

CAROLINE. Nothing. Nothing.

MARIE. No ... No! (*Backs off in fright.*)

CAROLINE. What's wrong? (*SHE takes the letter opener in her hand.*)

MARIE. Your daughter. You've killed your daughter.

CAROLINE. Oh, then she really was my daughter. How nice.

MARIE. You've killed her. (*Looks at the letter opener in horror.*)

CAROLINE. No, I haven't. It will all go away I'm sure. It will all go away. It always does. It will again. Sit down, Marie. We'll wait for David together.

(*CAROLINE sits down. MARIE sits next to her, weeping.*)

End of Scene 3

Scene 4

Later. The same day.
The Library.
STEFANIE's body is still lying there. MARIE is seated,
crying. Her white maid's apron is gone, her black dress
is now adorned with pearls. SIMON stands next to her,
his hand on her shoulder comforting her.
CAROLINE sits stunned. DAVID enters the room with
CHARLEY who is now in a trench coat. CAROLINE
does not take notice of either of them.

DAVID. *(Introducing Charley to all.)* This is Lieutenant
Anderson.

(SIMON and MARIE nod. CHARLEY goes to the body
and uncovers the face and then recovers it.)

CHARLEY. She's dead, all right.
DAVID. Yes, I told you she was.
CHARLEY. Sometimes they are, sometimes they
aren't. Okay, let's have it.
CAROLINE. *(Looking up at Charley.)* Do I know you?
CHARLEY. I don't think so.
CAROLINE. I'm sorry.
CHARLEY. Okay, let's get the story.

DAVID. Well, they never did get along. She was jealous. Very jealous.

CHARLEY. Who?

DAVID. (*Indicating Caroline.*) Her!

CHARLEY. Of what?

DAVID. Of her youth, of her future, and of our relationship.

CAROLINE. Yes, yes, it must be.

SIMON. It is.

MARIE. It's a sickness.

SIMON. Yes, a sickness. You see there's money in the family so it has to be a sickness.

MARIE. It's definitely a sickness. Believe me, Lieutenant, our daughter would not do something like this if there wasn't a sickness.

CAROLINE. Your daughter. I am not your daughter.

SIMON. Caroline!

CAROLINE. I am not her daughter. She's the maid! Marie is the maid.

SIMON. Caroline, please, your mother is upset enough.

CAROLINE. She is not my mother.

MARIE. My poor, poor little girl.

DAVID. You see what you're dealing with, Lieutenant.

CHARLEY. I'd rather not take sides till I know more.

CAROLINE. Good for you.

CHARLEY. Now you are the ...

DAVID. The victim's husband.

CAROLINE. David!

DAVID. What?

CAROLINE. That's another lie. You're my husband.

DAVID. Oh, Caroline ...

CAROLINE. It's true. That much I know is true. No matter what changes you've always been my husband.

DAVID. I am Stefanie's husband. Can't you get that through your head once and for all, Caroline. I am Stefanie's husband.

CHARLEY. *Was* Stefanie's husband. (*Indicates body.*) I believe this makes it *was*. Sorry.

DAVID. There was a tremendous rivalry between the two. I can't help but feel I was to blame.

SIMON. Nonsense, David.

DAVID. I was. I was. You see, Lieutenant, I was going to marry Caroline till she brought me home and introduced me to her daughter.

SIMON. As a 1940 comedy it would have made a wonderful romp.

MARIE. It was love at first sight. I'll attest to that.

DAVID. We ran away and got married. Caroline said she forgave us, but it's obvious now she hasn't.

CHARLEY. Now let me get this straight. (*Indicates Caroline.*) This woman who you were going to marry is now your mother-in-law?

DAVID. Correct!

CAROLINE. (*Laughing hysterically.*) Your mother-in-law? Oh, that's a good one. Thank God. I'm your mother-in-law, David. The maid is my mother. You're my son-in-law. For a minute, only for a minute, I thought this might be reality. But it still isn't, is it, David? Oh, I feel so much better.

SIMON. Please, dear.

CAROLINE. Oh, please, Father, play it out! Play it all out! Go ahead, all of you, play it out. Although this is the first time I've seen some levity in it. You surprise me,

David. I never suspected you of having a sense of humor. (*Laughs again.*) Oh, I really like this one. I do.

CHARLEY. You know, I was kind of hoping this would be a simple "Who done it!" I'm not very good with whackos.

CAROLINE. Well, now. You think you're dealing with madness, do you, Lieutenant? You might very well be right. The question is, whose? That's what you don't know yet, but I think I do. Right, David?

CHARLEY. Oh, shit!

(THEY all look at Charley for a moment. CAROLINE tries to restore dignity.)

CHARLEY. Sorry.

CAROLINE. The truth is it doesn't matter. Soon this will all change. Soon we'll all be into something else. Everyone of us. You will be Charley again and Marie will be the maid again and everyone will be everyone else again. (*To David.*) All except you and me, David. You and I are always the same. Caroline and David. Don't you think that's strange? Always Caroline and David. That should be the tip-off, shouldn't it?

DAVID. It amazes me how far some people will go to avoid the gas chamber.

SIMON. I'm learning not to be surprised by anything.

CAROLINE. I'm sorry to hear that, Father. It takes a certain zest out of life.

CHARLEY. I have a feeling I won't be getting home for dinner tonight.

CAROLINE. Don't be silly, Lieutenant Anderson, or whoever you are ... You can do whatever you want because this is only a moment which is sure to be replaced by another moment later on.

CHARLEY. Now wait a minute. There's been a murder here.

CAROLINE. I'm afraid not. Whoever is on that floor, will soon be gone and then come through a door as someone else because that's the way he's doing it.

CHARLEY. He?

CAROLINE. I'm getting on to this, David. Aren't you worried?

DAVID. Poor Caroline.

CAROLINE. No, shouldn't it be "poor Stefanie"? She's the one that's supposedly dead, right, David? Your wife, your stepdaughter, your lover. Where are the tears for her, David? There aren't any because nothing's really happened to her, has it? You cry when someone close to you dies, David. You cry. You didn't and I didn't.

DAVID. What makes you so sure you can?

CAROLINE. I can cry, David. I'm just not so sure what to cry about. (*Shakes Stefanie's body.*) Come on, Stefanie, get up. Up, up, up.

CHARLEY. Boy, that is sick, you know. Really sick.

DAVID. Sadistic is what I would call it.

CAROLINE. Of course, you would, David. The word suits you extremely well.

SIMON. Now, now, children, let's try to keep our dignity.

CAROLINE. (*To Charley.*) Lieutenant, may I talk to you alone?

CHARLEY. I don't know. (*To all.*) Is it all right? She doesn't have any more weapons on her?

CAROLINE. Of course, it's all right? Isn't it, David? It is all up to you, isn't it?

DAVID. (*A beat. Mysteriously.*) Call us if you need us, Lieutenant.

MARIE. (*Takes Caroline's hand.*) I want to be on your side. I honestly do.

CAROLINE. I know, Marie.

MARIE. (*Correcting her.*) It's Mother. It really is.

SIMON. We still love you, darling. Everyone loves you.

(MARIE, DAVID, and SIMON go off. The stage darkens. Only CAROLINE and Charley are lit.)

CHARLEY. (*Puzzled by the lighting affect.*) How did that happen?

CAROLINE. It's not natural, is it?

CHARLEY. No.

CAROLINE. I'm so glad you caught that. You see, Lieutenant, we are not real people.

CHARLEY. Oh boy.

CAROLINE. I mean, we are real people, but what we're going through is not real. This may come as a shock to you, but you see, we are all in his mind.

CHARLEY. We are?

CAROLINE. Yes.

CHARLEY. In his mind?

CAROLINE. Of course.

CHARLEY. In whose mind?

CAROLINE. David's! He toys with us. He puts us in these bizarre situations.

CHARLEY. Like you murdering your daughter?

CAROLINE. Yes, except you don't really think she is my daughter? I mean she can't be. If she was, don't you think I would be more upset than I am?

CHARLEY. I'd say you're pretty upset.

CAROLINE. You would? Well, that may be because you don't know me. But then again, you really do, don't you? I mean not as a detective but as the real you.

CHARLEY. Oh, Christ ...

CAROLINE. You must know who you really are. Think, Charley, think.

CHARLEY. Charley? How did you know my first name?

CAROLINE. You've got to think before it starts to cloud up again. Before he changes it. You've got to show strength, your will, to gain control. That is the only way we can break him.

CHARLEY. Look, lady, I don't know about you but I'm as real as hell. I eat, I sleep, I make a living ...

CAROLINE. I swear, Charley, we are not in reality.

CAROLINE. (*Goes to body.*) Watch! Just watch! (*Shakes the body.*) Stefanie! Stefanie! Get up. Get up.

CHARLEY. I never seen anything like you, lady.

CAROLINE. Get up, Stefanie. (*To Charley.*) Children are so uncooperative these days.

CHARLEY. Listen, maybe I should have asked you sooner, but are you in therapy?

CAROLINE. She's alive. She's not dead. (*Shaking Stefanie.*) Talk to him, Stefanie. Make him understand. Look! She's been stabbed and there's no blood. That's another thing. There's never any blood. (*To Charley.*) She'll get up. You'll see.

CHARLEY. Lady, right now all I see is you and me and soon it's just gonna be you. I'll be in touch. (*HE turns to go.*)

CAROLINE. No. No, please don't go. Don't go! Please! Please! She won't get up because he doesn't want her to. Don't go!

DAVID. (*Enters.*) Caroline! What's wrong? I heard you shouting.

CAROLINE. (*Hysterical.*) It's yours, isn't it? It's *your* mind. I know it's *your* mind.

DAVID. What are you talking about?

CAROLINE. You're the one. You're doing it. We are all in your mind. I've got to put a stop to this.

STEFANIE. (*Sitting up.*) Use the letter opener. (*SHE hands Caroline the letter opener that was lying next to her.*) It always changes things.

CAROLINE. Yes.

CHARLEY. (*Indicating Stefanie.*) She's alive!

(*CAROLINE grabs the letter opener and runs towards David.*)

DAVID. (*Frightened.*) Caroline.

CAROLINE. (*SHE raises the letter opener.*) No, I can't. I don't want to. I'm not going to.

STEFANIE. Do it! You did it to me. You can do it to him.

CAROLINE. No! No! No!

(*SHE drops the letter opener and falls into David's arms and holds him. STEFANIE plays dead again.*)

CAROLINE. Darling! Darling, David.
DAVID. It's all right. It's all right.
CAROLINE. I need you.

*(CHARLEY goes over to inspect Stefanie. HE lifts her
arm. It's limp.)*

CHARLEY. *(In disbelief.)* She's dead again.
SIMON. *(Enters hurriedly.)* Oh, my God, what's the
matter now?
CAROLINE. Tell him it's nothing, David. Tell him
nothing is wrong and maybe it won't be.
DAVID. Simon, nothing is wrong.
CAROLINE. *(In David's arms.)* Oh, thank you, David.
I love you.
DAVID. And I love you, Caroline.

(MARIE enters as the maid.)

MARIE. Excuse me, Mr. Ogden.
DAVID. Yes, Marie?
MARIE. Lieutenant Anderson is here.
CAROLINE. Oh no.
CHARLEY. Who?
MARIE. Lieutenant Anderson.
DAVID. Send him in. We've been expecting him.
CHARLEY. Hey, wait. I am here.

(MARIE starts out. DAVID picks up the letter opener.)

CHARLEY. I am Lieutenant Anderson.
DAVID. Not for long.

*(HE plunges the letter opener into Charley's stomach.
CHARLEY moans, doubles up in horror, clutches his
stomach and falls back onto the sofa.)*

CHARLEY. Oh, my God, he stabbed me.
SIMON. So he did.
CAROLINE. *(Terrified.)* David!
DAVID. *(Hands her the letter opener and takes her in
his arms.)* Relax, darling. Everything's going to be fine.
CAROLINE. *(Looking at the letter opener.)* It's not.
It's not.
CHARLEY. There's no blood! I've been stabbed and
there's no blood. Okay, Mrs. Ogden, I believe you. I'll
take the case.

*(HE collapses. CAROLINE breaks away from David, goes
to Charley and throws her arms around him.)*

CAROLINE. Thank God. He's going to help me! He's
going to help me!

CURTAIN

End of ACT I

ACT II

Scene 1

TIME: Later that evening.
PLACE: The Library.
CAROLINE and CHARLEY are seated having tea.
CAROLINE is now very well composed. Stefanie's body is gone.

CHARLEY. I can't get over that Boy, did that feel real. Right smack in the stomach.

CAROLINE. I should have known he'd try something like that.

CHARLEY. Like what?

CAROLINE. Making me seem the mad one. Threatening my credibility.

CHARLEY. (*Picks up book on table.*) Oh, Kurt Vonnegut. Do you like him?

CAROLINE. Yes. His imagination fascinates me. What about you?

CHARLEY. No. Don't care for him at all. I'm strictly an Agatha Christie man. I like to have things laid out more, you know, black and white, where there are definite answers for everything somewhere in the book.

CAROLINE. It is neater, isn't it?

CHARLEY. It really is. I like that.

CAROLINE. I'm surprised then, Lieutenant, that you find this particular situation very hard to accept.

CHARLEY. That this is all taking place in someone's mind? No. One thing I've learned and it's probably basic as hell ...

CAROLINE. I'd love to hear it.

CHARLEY. It takes all kinds.

CAROLINE. Yes. You could be right. At first it was devastating, the way he could manipulate the situations. I started to lose focus. I was practically what you might call a basket case.

CHARLEY. At the very least.

CAROLINE. God, how he'd toy with me. Each time letting me go farther and farther before climaxing with some horrifying trauma.

CHARLEY. Drama?

CAROLINE. Trauma. Brought on by the drama. But I'm getting on to it, and soon, maybe soon, I can beat him at his game.

CHARLEY. It's a cruel game masterminded by an insane mind.

CAROLINE. Exactly.

CHARLEY. I hope so.

CAROLINE. But that's how we'll get him. An insane mind is a flawed mind. That's how we escape. Through the flaw. Back to reality.

CHARLEY. Which this isn't.

CAROLINE. No, I'm afraid not.

(STEFANIE, as the maid, enters with a tea tray.)

STEFANIE. Excuse me, Mrs. Ogden. I brought some fresh tea.

CAROLINE. Thank you, Marie.

CHARLEY. Boy, this is some swell house. Is this the way it is in real life?

CAROLINE. Yes. It's been in the family for years.

CHARLEY. Old money. I wouldn't be surprised if that's what your husband's after.

CAROLINE. Really. That simple a thing?

CHARLEY. Yeah. Hey, maybe they'll make me a Captain for this.

(STEFANIE has poured the tea and starts out.)

CAROLINE. Thank you, Marie.

STEFANIE. You're welcome, Mrs. Ogden. By the way I won't be taking my day off this week. Under the circumstances it just isn't possible.

CAROLINE. I understand.

(STEFANIE exits.)

CAROLINE. Did you notice?

CHARLEY. Notice what?

CAROLINE. Marie. Don't you remember her?

CHARLEY. Should I?

CAROLINE. She was the dead body when you arrived.

CHARLEY. She was?

CAROLINE. Yes, my daughter, the maid, David's wife and secretary.

CHARLEY. You saw four bodies?

CAROLINE. No. It was the same body. Her function kept changing. He can do that. By the way, did you notice it was gone?

CHARLEY. What?

CAROLINE. The body.

CHARLEY. (*Peers over to area.*) Oh, my goodness, it is. What happened to it?

CAROLINE. It just served you tea.

CHARLEY. This does it. I gotta go. I'm history. (*Rises.*) See you, lady, and maybe not.

CAROLINE. Don't Lieutenant. You said you'd help. (*Blocking his way.*) Now, we've got to hurry. I don't know how long he'll permit our alliance to last. But somewhere in all this, there's a way out. A door to reality. I'm sure of it.

CHARLEY. Boy, you tell one hell of a story. Yet, I know something is screwy. I mean, here I am drinking tea and I hate tea. But it's so crazy. I just don't know how much of it I can buy.

CAROLINE. May I ask you something, Lieutenant? Your wife ...

CHARLEY. Millie?

CAROLINE. If that's her name. What's she like?

CHARLEY. Just a plain ordinary wife.

CAROLINE. Your children. How many?

CHARLEY. Two.

CAROLINE. What are their names? (*The pace quickens.*)

CHARLEY. Johnny, Jane, why?

CAROLINE. How old?

CHARLEY. Ten and eleven.

CAROLINE. How long have you been married? What's the color of her eyes? Her hair? Where did you meet?

CHARLEY. I ... I ...

CAROLINE. Your address. Quick, your address.

CHARLEY. 316 ... 18 ... No, 16 ... Yes, that's it ... 16.

CAROLINE. 16 what?

CHARLEY. (*Amazed.*) 16 ... 16 ... I don't know.

CAROLINE. See! See he can't think that fast. Maybe that's the flaw, the way out.

CHARLEY. (*Rises.*) Look, I have to go.

CAROLINE. No, don't. He wants you to go. Don't.

CHARLEY. I have to.

CAROLINE. A picture!

CHARLEY. What?

CAROLINE. Do you have a picture of her?

(*CAROLINE pushes Charley down on a chair, holding him with her knee across his lap.*)

CHARLEY. Of who?

CAROLINE. Your wife.

CHARLEY. Sure.

CAROLINE. Let me see it. Quickly.

CHARLEY. (*Takes out wallet and opens to a photo.*) I really have to go.

CAROLINE. (*Takes wallet and examines photo.*) This is her?

CHARLEY. Look, I know my wife.

CAROLINE. It's me.

CHARLEY. What?

CAROLINE. That picture is of me.

CHARLEY. (*Takes wallet and examines photo.*) Holy God. It is you. If my wife finds out she'll kill me. I don't get it. I just don't get it. Why would I have your picture ...

CAROLINE. He wants to make it more exciting, don't you see? Maybe that's why he's given us this time. Oh, please, I can't be in this alone anymore. I need help, Charley. I need help. You've got to stay strong. That's the only way we can beat him.

CHARLEY. (*Rises. Puts wallet away.*) I have to go.

CAROLINE. No, please, don't. I need you, desperately. You can't leave me to that bastard.

CHARLEY. (*Pats her hair. His attitude suddenly changes.*) Sweet wonderful Caroline. To think that there is someone who hates you so much that the only way to get you is in his mind. What have you done to him, Caroline? Do you know what you've done?

CAROLINE. He's making you say that, isn't he? That's not you. See, he's making you say that. Why are you calling me Caroline? Why not Mrs. Ogden? See, something is happening to you, Lieutenant.

CHARLEY. (*As the Lieutenant.*) I've gotta go. I really do.

CAROLINE. No, please, don't Charley. If ever you loved me, don't go.

CHARLEY. Why would I love you? I just met you.

CAROLINE. I'm not mad. I swear I'm not mad. We were married once. We meant something to each other. It's you I always loved. I'm sure of it. Don't go. I need someone.

CHARLEY. I'm sorry, lady. This whole day has been pretty upsetting.

(As CHARLEY exits HE passes SIMON entering.)

SIMON. Hello.

CHARLEY. Goodbye. (*HE exits.*)

SIMON. I wanted to see how you were doing.

CAROLINE. I've got to get away, Simon. I'm living a nightmare.

SIMON. I know. I would help if I could but it just isn't possible.

CAROLINE. I'd do anything. I mean it. Anything.

SIMON. You could use the letter opener.

CAROLINE. On David? What's the use. It doesn't work.

SIMON. On yourself. (*HE hands her the letter opener.*) We'd all understand, Caroline. And it might be the answer.

(CAROLINE examines the letter opener and toys with the idea of using it, as SIMON slowly exits off stage. SHE then puts it down.)

CAROLINE. No. I can't. That's what he wants me to do. I won't. I won't.

(SHE puts the letter opener on a table, sinks to a chair and buries her face in her hands. DAVID enters, looks at her for a beat and smiles tenderly.)

DAVID. Caroline! Caroline!

CAROLINE. What? Huh?

DAVID. You've fallen asleep.

CAROLINE. I haven't.

DAVID. Of course, you have, and the Clarks will be here any minute.

CAROLINE. The ... The Clarks.

DAVID. We're going to the theatre with them, dear. What's wrong with you?

CAROLINE. The ... Clarks?

DAVID. Caroline, look at me. Wake up. Come on, please, darling, we'll be late.

CAROLINE. Yes. Maybe you're right. Maybe I was asleep. I must try to remember who the Clarks are.

(SOUND: O.S. DOORBELL.)

DAVID. My God, that's probably them.

CAROLINE. David, was I really sleeping?

DAVID. Soundly. I almost hated to wake you.

CAROLINE. Yes, I was sleeping. I must have been. Of course, I was. *(Relieved.)* And everything seems so good.

DAVID. *(Confused.)* Everything is good, Caroline. Why shouldn't it be?

CAROLINE. Yes, yes, you're right. I'm fine now. I know it.

MARIE. *(Enters.)* Mr. and Mrs. Clark are here.

(CHARLEY and STEFANIE enter in evening clothes. THEY go to David and Caroline.)

STEFANIE. David.
DAVID. Stefanie.
CHARLEY. Caroline.
DAVID. Charley.

CHARLEY and STEFANIE. *(With outstretched hands to Caroline.)* Well?

DAVID. *(To Caroline.)* Well?

CAROLINE. *(A beat; stunned.)* It's so nice to see you all again.

BLACKOUT

End of Scene 1

ACT II

Scene 2

Later that evening.
The Library.
CAROLINE, DAVID, CHARLEY and STEFANIE. DAVID and CHARLEY are removing wraps from CAROLINE and STEFANIE.

STEFANIE. I loved it. I absolutely loved it. I don't know why people keep knocking the theatre. I don't know when I've had a more enjoyable evening.

CHARLEY. How could you find it enjoyable? It ended in a castration.

STEFANIE. I don't care. At least there was depth to it. I happen to love depth. Especially in the theatre.

DAVID. It made you think. It really did.

STEFANIE. Yes, it did. That's probably the reason why it's not doing so well. People just hate to think in the theatre. Charley especially. But I do, I really do. How did you like it, Caroline? You've been so quiet all evening.

CAROLINE. Oh, it was nice ... very nice.

STEFANIE. Well, I loved it. I absolutely loved it. And the sets. I just loved the sets, too.

CHARLEY. It was one big wall.

STEFANIE. But oh, what a statement.

DAVID. Are you all right, Caroline?

CAROLINE. Yes, of course. Why do you ask?

DAVID. I'm concerned.

CAROLINE. I feel fine. Really, I do.

DAVID. Really?

CAROLINE. Yes, really. Does it surprise you?

DAVID. Why should you say that?

(An awkward beat between them.)

STEFANIE. Well, I loved it.

CAROLINE. Will you stop it already.

DAVID. How about some drinks?

CHARLEY. What the hell do you think we're here for?

STEFANIE. I'll have some sherry.

CHARLEY. Make that two.

DAVID. Caroline?

CAROLINE. I don't know. What do I usually have?

DAVID. I don't know.

CAROLINE. You don't? Why not?

DAVID. Well, you're not very consistent. It's been one of your strong points.

CAROLINE. Do I drink sherry?

DAVID. I don't know. On occasion, I would assume you do. Don't you?

CAROLINE. Maybe.

DAVID. We both seem to be floundering on this particular subject, don't we?

CAROLINE. You would think that after all these years you would know what I drink.

DAVID. Yes, you would, wouldn't you?

CAROLINE. How many years, David?

DAVID. What?

CAROLINE. How many years have we been together?

DAVID. Been together or married?

CAROLINE. Either.

STEFANIE. Oh, come on, Caroline. You don't think he's forgotten?

CAROLINE. Do you know?

STEFANIE. Of course, we know. We attended the wedding.

DAVID. Caroline, there is something wrong. Why are you behaving so strangely?

STEFANIE. You're not still upset about that gypsy in the lobby?

CHARLEY. Oh, come on, Stefanie. It had to be a little unnerving. I mean, how would you like it if some weird, old crone handed *you* the Queen of Spades and then disappeared into the crowd?

DAVID. Four sherrys, how's that?

(DAVID pours four drinks. STEFANIE picks up a book from the table.)

STEFANIE. *The Good Earth.* I haven't read Pearl Buck since high school.

DAVID. Caroline's been reading everything she can about the old China and the new China.

STEFANIE. Oh, of course. For her trip.

CAROLINE. My trip?

DAVID. God, I wish I could go with her, but I'm such a terrible traveler. *(Passes out drinks.)*

STEFANIE. That's Caroline, always the adventuress. But I guess with her money, why not? How long will you be away this time?

CAROLINE. I ... I ...

DAVID. Eight weeks I believe.

STEFANIE. My God, if I left Charles alone for eight weeks he'd kill me. How can you stand it, David?

DAVID. It does get lonely at times.

CAROLINE. *(Softly, confused.)* I'm not going to China.

DAVID. What's that, dear?

CAROLINE. I said I'm not going to China.

DAVID. Of course, you are, dear. *(To Stefanie and Charley.)* Frankly, I don't like Caroline's being away one bit, but you know what a strong willed person she is.

CAROLINE. I have no interest at all in China. Really, David.

(DAVID and STEFANIE pay no attention to her. CHARLEY eyes her tentatively.)

DAVID. I will miss her every minute she's away.

STEFANIE. Oh, come on, David. I've yet to meet a married man who didn't appreciate a few weeks of bachelorhood now and then.

DAVID. No, no, really. I don't.

STEFANIE. (*Teasing.*) Not just a little.

DAVID. Well, maybe a little.

STEFANIE. How would you like to call me for lunch one day?

DAVID. That might be very nice.

STEFANIE. I would make sure it was.

(THEY look at each other and then kiss.)

DAVID. Would you like to go for a walk in the garden?

STEFANIE. (*To Charley.*) You don't mind, do you, Charley?

CHARLEY. No, not at all.

(DAVID and STEFANIE exit, holding hands.)

CHARLEY. (*Calling.*) Have a nice time.

(CHARLEY and CAROLINE are alone.)

CAROLINE. How could you permit that?

CHARLEY. It's okay. I'm back again.

CAROLINE. What?

CHARLEY. I'm with you a hundred percent. You see, I did what you said. I stayed strong. I kept a fix on things ... on what was before. That's the key, you know, what was before. Anyway, I don't think he was concentrating that hard. Especially at the theatre, because I could still faintly remember who I was when we talked for the first time ... I think it was a ... a detective.

CAROLINE. Yes. Lieutenant Anderson.

CHARLEY. Yes, that's him. Who I am ... or was. I'm going to do my best to help you, Mrs. Ogden. I really am and I think I can pull it off. I seem to get more freedom than you. Maybe that's because you're his central character and I'm not that important. Boy, that's a bummer for my self image isn't it?

CAROLINE. You really want to help me?

CHARLEY. It's certainly the romantic thing to do, isn't it? Besides, aren't detectives supposed to help, if that's, in fact, what I am. I may not be, you know. I'm probably not. Although I do love being one. I wonder if it was ever a fantasy of mine.

CAROLINE. No, not that I recall.

CHARLEY. Yes. Yes, you would know. I remember you told me I was your husband. I guess that was before Mr. Ogden.

CAROLINE. Yes.

CHARLEY. It seems strange because I am a lot younger than he is. Why would you dump me? Because I don't think I would dump you.

CAROLINE. Really?

CHARLEY. Probably not.

CAROLINE. I don't know what happened. He keeps it so muddy for me. But I do know you've always meant something important to me.

CHARLEY. That's good. I like that. Anyway, I have a plan that I think will work. I thought about it at the theatre. I hated the play you know. Much too real for my taste. I was in the mood for escapism. Anyway, we've got to think of this mind we're in as kind of a small, seething volcanic island, active bubbling, menacing on the top, yet, on the bottom lush with trees and ferns. As long as it's seething, nothing happens, it remains the same. But once it blows, whamo, all hell breaks loose. And that's when we make our move. We run down to the lush part, grab a motor boat and take off. How does that sound?

CAROLINE. I am so disappointed, I can't begin to tell you.

CHARLEY. You're missing the point. You see what we've got to do is push his mind all the way. We get it to explode. Once it goes, blows apart, there'll be an opening for us. We just have to trigger the explosion, don't you see? And with a crazy mind there are all kinds of ways to do that. Listen to me, Caroline. I know what I'm talking about.

CAROLINE. (*Turns away and starts to laugh.*) He did it. He did it again. He gave me some hope and then took it away.

CHARLEY. No, no. I won't let him. I'll do it. I'll get you out of here ... I swear I will. Did ... did you really love me?

CAROLINE. Yes. I think so.

CHARLEY. A little? A lot?

CAROLINE. Love is love. I never thought there was a quantity to it.

CHARLEY. I like that. That's very nice. What other memories to you have of me?

CAROLINE. I don't know. Vague ones. But all with feelings. Feelings that I somehow had for you, that I never had for David.

CHARLEY. Still?

CAROLINE. (*A beat.*) Yes. Still.

CHARLEY. I like that.

CAROLINE. And yours? What are your memories?

CHARLEY. I don't know. At times I catch flashes of them, moments, but before I can get a grip on them they fade away.

CAROLINE. They said you died.

CHARLEY. I can't remember that. But then who would want to?

CAROLINE. I hope it's not true.

CHARLEY. Me, too.

CAROLINE. Hold me, Charley. Hold me. I want to be in your arms.

CHARLEY. (*Takes her in his arms.*) It's a very normal reaction if we can use that word around here at all.

(*THEY embrace for a beat and then CAROLINE breaks away.*)

CAROLINE. Shall I make you another drink?

CHARLEY. Sure. But not Sherry. I don't really like it very much.

CAROLINE. You used to drink scotch. On the rocks.

CHARLEY. Really?

CAROLINE. You don't remember?

CHARLEY. No. But now that you mention it, it sounds good. What else did I used to do?

CAROLINE. It's funny. It's starting to come back. You used to get drunk and do silly things and be loud and gamble and make me laugh and cry.

CHARLEY. Really, me? And what were you like? Were you really like you are now?

CAROLINE. How is that? (*Hands him his drink.*)

CHARLEY. So unprotected, so afraid, so defenseless.

CAROLINE. I don't know. Sometimes I think I'm very strong. Bitchy in a way, then I don't know.

CHARLEY. (*Sips his drink.*) Hey, this is good. (*Sips a long one.*)

CAROLINE. You even drink like Charley. You shouldn't. Sometimes he got nasty.

CHARLEY. No kidding.

CAROLINE. Sometimes.

CHARLEY. Look, why do you think all this is happening to you?

CAROLINE. I don't know.

CHARLEY. Oh, come on. By now you must have some idea.

CAROLINE. I really don't.

CHARLEY. There has to be a tremendous amount of hatred involved somewhere.

CAROLINE. Yes. I think that's true.

CHARLEY. Or love. We've all known about relationships like that.

CAROLINE. I don't think it's love.

CHARLEY. It could be.

CAROLINE. No, it's not love.

CHARLEY. (*Irked. Louder.*) It could be.

(*CAROLINE looks at him for a beat.*)

CHARLEY. I ... I'm sorry. (*Finishes his drink and pours himself another.*)

CAROLINE. I know hate, Charley, but I also know love. I loved you, Charley. But you never loved me. You never did, you know.

CHARLEY. (*Doesn't want to hear this.*) Please.

CAROLINE. You didn't. I mean when you were the real Charley. You used me, you used my money. But I didn't seem to care. And women, you were always involved with women. I caught you with several.

CHARLEY. At one time?

CAROLINE. Sometimes.

CHARLEY. God, I wish I knew me then. I'm straight as an arrow now.

CAROLINE. You seem to be.

CHARLEY. Well, sometimes a person matures in death. We need more ice. Never mind. I'll take it straight.

CAROLINE. What do you think of her?

CHARLEY. Who?

CAROLINE. Stefanie. The wife David gave you.

CHARLEY. Oh, she's very pretty.

CAROLINE. A bit young for you, don't you think?

CHARLEY. No, I think about right.

CAROLINE. I'm twenty years older.

CHARLEY. Which is good 'cause I can fit nicely right in the middle. (*Looks off into the gardens.*) I ran off with someone, didn't I? Was it her? Was it Stefanie?

CAROLINE. You don't remember?

CHARLEY. I'm trying to. I'm really trying.

CAROLINE. It wouldn't have worked. She didn't have a penny and you with your gambling and other habits, it was a hopeless situation from the beginning.

CHARLEY. (*Turns on her angrily.*) It could have worked. It could have this time. We were going to South America. I had a job there. I just needed thirty thousand dollars from you, Caroline. Just thirty thousand to pay some debts and start fresh.

CAROLINE. You were self-destructive, Charley.

CHARLEY. I would have worked hard. I could have made it. You never believed in me.

CAROLINE. You were limited in character, at the end, even you saw that.

CHARLEY. (*Goes towards her menacingly.*) You should have given me the money, Caroline. It would have changed everything.

CAROLINE. Keep away from me, Charley. I warn you.

CHARLEY. I told you my life was in danger. I told you!

CAROLINE. I thought it was another lie. You always lied to me. I didn't know anymore.

CHARLEY. I want that money, Caroline. I deserve it. I earned it. (*Twists her arm.*)

CAROLINE. Let me go. It's over. Done. You're reliving something that's no more.

CHARLEY. You owe it to me!

CAROLINE. Stop it, Charley. You're hurting me.

(As CHARLEY continues to hurt her, CAROLINE grabs the letter opener from the table to defend herself.)

MARIE. (*Enters with an ice bucket.*) I thought you might be needing more ice, Mrs. Ogden.

(CHARLEY snaps out of it. HE releases Caroline.)

CAROLINE. (*Composing herself.*) Yes. Thank you. We do, as-a-matter-of-fact.

MARIE. I thought so.

(MARIE puts the ice bucket down. CHARLEY sits on a chair, disgusted with himself.)

MARIE. Do you think you'll be needing anything else?

CAROLINE. No, Marie. Thank you.

MARIE. *(Looks at Charley with scorn.)* Would you like some coffee, Mr. Clark?

CHARLEY. No. No thanks. It makes me nervous.

MARIE. *(To Charley; mysterious.)* It's all so very intriguing, isn't it, Mr. Clark?

(CHARLEY nods. MARIE exits.)

CHARLEY. *(Ashamed.)* If she hadn't come in I would have broken your arm. If she hadn't come in, I could have hurt you badly. That's not me. I don't like that in me. I'm sorry.

CAROLINE. *(Puts down the letter opener and runs her fingers through his hair.)* You used to hit me a lot. Yet there were times I didn't mind.

CHARLEY. *(Rising.)* I need another drink.

CAROLINE. No, please, don't. No more.

(CAROLINE kisses Charley. DAVID and STEFANIE enter.)

CAROLINE. I loved you, Charley. I loved only you.

DAVID. Really, Caroline. Then why did you kill him?

CHARLEY. *(A beat; shocked.)* You ... it was you?

CAROLINE. No.

DAVID. It was nothing very original. A letter opener in the back. He was going to leave you.

CAROLINE. I ... I didn't. I couldn't have.

CHARLEY. You killed me. That's why I'm so young. You killed me. I was in my prime.

STEFANIE. Look, let's go home, Charley. I don't want to hear this I was having a good time until now.

CAROLINE. Don't go. You said you'd help me, Charley, remember?

CHARLEY. You ... You killed me.

CAROLINE. (*Recalling*.) You can't believe him. You were going to stay strong.

CHARLEY. I loved someone else. You wouldn't let me go.

(*SIMON and MARIE enter from the shadows.*)

SIMON. You killed him, Caroline.

MARIE. I'm afraid you did, dear.

DAVID. A messy affair. It made all the papers.

CHARLEY. (*Confused*.) She did it. She really did it. Yes ... Yes ... the letter opener. That's what she used.

CAROLINE. It had to be self defense. That's the only way I would have killed you, Charley, in self defense. I loved you, Charley, and you loved me.

STEFANIE. You never loved anyone, but yourself, Mother. You shouldn't have stopped us. You should have let us go.

CAROLINE. It was you. He was running off with you. No, no it wasn't that way. It wasn't that way at all. That's David making us think it was. Tell them, David. It's you who's making us act this way and say these things.

(SIMON brings out a small medical bag and takes out a hypodermic needle.)

DAVID. I did so much for you, Caroline, but you wouldn't accept it. I've shown you more tenderness and concern than anyone else could possibly show you. And for what? All I ever heard from you was "Charley! I love only Charley." Well, goddamn it, you should have loved me.

SIMON. You should have, Caroline. (*HE hands the needle to David.*)

MARIE. It would have made things easier for all of us.

STEFANIE. We wouldn't be here now if you had.

DAVID. (*Slowly coming towards her with the needle.*) It's too late, Caroline. Now it's too late. Now you've made me loathe you, despise you, detest you. You made it all so painful, Caroline. So impossibly painful.

CAROLINE. Help me, Charley.

STEFANIE. He's dead, Mother. Charley's dead.

CAROLINE. He's not! I know he's not! And stop calling me mother.

MARIE. Easy, dear, easy.

CAROLINE. You just want me to believe he's dead. You want me to believe that I did it.

DAVID. There was blood, don't you remember. So much blood.

CAROLINE. Keep away from me.

CHARLEY. (*HE wants to help. HE can't move.*) David! For God's sake stop it!

DAVID. Stay out of this.

(STEFANIE, MARIE and SIMON go to CAROLINE and hold her so that SHE can't run from David.)

STEFANIE. David knows what he's doing, Mother.

MARIE. It's much easier if you don't fight him.

SIMON. He's been so patient. We all have, Caroline.

CAROLINE. Don't let him do this to me, Charley! Don't let him!

CHARLEY. (*Confused panic.*) I don't know what to do? (*Held back by an invisible force, HE's unable to help.*)

DAVID. (*Injecting Caroline in the arm.*) Relax, darling. Relax.

CAROLINE. (*Weakened. SHE sinks to a chair.*) We've got to break him, Charley. Help me.

CHARLEY. I want to. I want to.

CAROLINE. We've got to stop his mind from thinking this. Help me!

CHARLEY. (*Determined.*) I will. I'll find a way! I swear I will.

DAVID. (*Sits on sofa triumphantly.*) No one can help you now, Caroline. No one can. I'm in control here. Total control! Total control!

(*CAROLINE sinks into unconsciousness. CHARLEY looks on helplessly. The stage lightens on DAVID and then goes to BLACK.*)

End of Scene 2

ACT II

Scene 3

Library — Night .

The stage is now BRIGHT. A wicker basket containing a tennis racket and a croquet mallet has been placed at stage left near the French doors.

CAROLINE is asleep on a chair a book on her lap. DAVID is sipping a glass of wine. CAROLINE wakens.

CAROLINE. Oh, I fell asleep. It's the new Norman Mailer book. I just can't get through it. What time is it?

DAVID. Almost eight.

CAROLINE. What have you been doing all this time?

DAVID. Just sipping wine and looking at you and telling myself how lucky I am.

CAROLINE. (*Goes to him and kisses him.*) How lucky we are, David. How lucky I am to have finally found someone as wonderful as you.

MARIE. (*Enters with a tea tray.*) Mr. Ogden said I should bring some tea at eight just in case you woke up.

CAROLINE. You think of everything for me, don't you, David? Thank you, Marie.

(STEFANIE enters in a new dress.)

STEFANIE. Mother, you must fix the back of this dress. The zipper is stuck again, and I'm being picked up at eight.

CAROLINE. It's that natty material always catching on the clasp. You look just beautiful, Stefanie, doesn't she, David?

DAVID. Almost as beautiful as her mother.

STEFANIE. Oh, David. Does he ever say the wrong thing, Mother?

DAVID. Never. Absolutely never.

MARIE. Would you care for some tea, Mr. Ogden?

DAVID. No. Maybe another glass of that wine, Marie.

MARIE. The Bordeaux.

DAVID. Yes, thank you. Sixty-six was such a marvelous year for Bordeaux.

CAROLINE. I'm so glad.

(MARIE pours the wine for him. SIMON enters.)

SIMON. Hello, everyone.

CAROLINE. Hello, Father.

DAVID. Hello, Simon.

STEFANIE. Hello, Grandfather.

SIMON. I thought I'd pick out a good book before I go to bed.

CAROLINE. Michner has a new one out.

SIMON. No, thanks. I'd be worried all through it that the Good Lord would take me before I got to the end.

STEFANIE. Oh, Grandfather. You are precious.

SIMON. It comes with experience.

MARIE. What a wonderful family you are. What a simply wonderful family you are. It's a blessing to be part of it.

CAROLINE. Thank you, Marie.

MARIE. Thank you.

(MARIE exits. CAROLINE has the dress zipped up.)

CAROLINE. There. That should do it. Let me look at you.

(STEFANIE spins about.)

DAVID. Perfect. Absolutely perfect.

STEFANIE. *(Kissing David.)* Goodnight, David. *(Kisses Caroline.)* Goodnight, Mother. I'll be home early. *(Kisses Simon.)* Goodnight, Grandfather.

CAROLINE. Oh, David, I'm so incredibly happy.

DAVID. *(Sitting in a chair.)* Yes, things have worked out quite nicely for us, haven't they darling?

(Suddenly the garden doors fling open and CHARLEY enters, wielding a knife.)

CHARLEY. *(Screaming.)* David!

(HE plunges the knife into David's chest. CAROLINE and STEFANIE scream as DAVID sinks dead in the chair.)

CAROLINE. David! Oh, no, Charley, you've killed him.

CHARLEY. You were right, you know. It was him. He was doing this to us.

CAROLINE. What are you talking about?

CHARLEY. I did what you said. I stayed strong. And now we can get out. It *was* his mind, Caroline. We were all in *his* mind.

MARIE. (*Entering.*) What happened? I heard screams.
STEFANIE. Charley's escaped and killed David.
MARIE. My God! My God!
CHARLEY. Escaped? Escaped from where?
STEFANIE. The hospital.
CHARLEY. What hospital?
STEFANIE. The one for the criminally insane, Charley. Where you've been for the past eight years.

(*A SPOT gets brighter on CHARLEY as it dims down on the rest of the stage.*)

CHARLEY. Oh, my God. It was me! It was my mind! It was my mind!

(*The LIGHT goes out on Charley. CHARLEY and CAROLINE leave the stage. The LIGHTS go up and SIMON, STEFANIE and MARIE are seated on the sofa reading books. DAVID is still in the chair in his death position. HE slowly comes to life, looks at the three reading, smiles, gets up and goes to the wine decanter and pours himself a glass of wine.*)

DAVID. Wine anyone?
SIMON. No thank you, David.
MARIE. Not for me.
STEFANIE. Pass.
DAVID. What are you guys reading?
SIMON. *Heidi.*
STEFANIE. *The Wizard of Oz.*
MARIE. *Robin Hood and his Merry Men.*

DAVID. Good books. Safe books. No psychological twists. Just a nice straight path. No detours. No missing bricks. No puddles to jump.

STEFANIE. And when you finish them, you finish them.

SIMON. You know who the heroes are, you know who the villains are.

MARIE. Black and white are such wonderful colors.

DAVID. Yes, but then again, isn't a rainbow more interesting?

STEFANIE. Maybe. But there are some of us who need answers.

(CHARLEY enters.)

SIMON. How is she, Charley?

CHARLEY. I have never seen anyone so tormented in my life. She really believes I killed David. Poor thing. I had to strap her to the bed. That's what you wanted me to do, right, David?

DAVID. Yes, that's fine. Was she sad about my death?

CHARLEY. Actually, no. In fact, she seemed a bit relieved which I find totally understandable. She really loved me though, didn't she, David?

DAVID. Yes, she did. Wine?

CHARLEY. A little scotch. I'll help myself. *(Pours some scotch for himself.)* What did happen to me, David?

DAVID. I guess you deserve to know. When Caroline found out you were leaving her for Stefanie she put this in your back. *(Holds up letter opener.)* You died just about where you're standing now.

CHARLEY. Then it wasn't self defense?

DAVID. Not actually, but after the awful picture her battery of lawyers painted of you, the jury felt it was close enough.

SIMON. For some reason, when the rich commit murder it's always considered more a misdemeanor than a felony.

STEFANIE. And what about me?

DAVID. You did very well. You married a real estate agent you met at Charley's funeral. The two of you practically own Rhode Island.

CHARLEY. Boy, are you lucky.

(During the following, DAVID puts on a tennis sweater.)

MARIE. And Simon and I? Are we happy, David?

DAVID. Yes, I guess so. If you'd like I'll ask you next time I see you to make sure.

SIMON. That would be nice.

STEFANIE. What about you, David? Are you happy?

DAVID. Now and then.

CHARLEY. When, David? In fantasy or reality? Or can't you tell the difference anymore either?

DAVID. What's that supposed to mean?

SIMON. It means get on with it. Be the man you want to be. All you're succeeding in doing is hating yourself as much as you hate her. It's not a healthy situation and frankly we're all getting a bit worn.

STEFANIE. Free yourself, David. You deserve it and so does Caroline.

DAVID. Maybe one day I will.

CHARLEY. Sure. Sure, David.

DAVID. *(Louder.)* I said, maybe one day I will.

*(CAROLINE enters wearing tennis clothes and carrying a
racket. SHE is arrogant, cold.)*

CAROLINE. David?
DAVID. Yes.
CAROLINE. Who are you talking to?
DAVID. No one, dear.
CAROLINE. I heard you talking to someone.
DAVID. No, no one, dear.
CAROLINE. *(Curious.)* Are you all right?
DAVID. Yes, of course.
CAROLINE. Good. It's a lovely day for tennis, isn't it?
DAVID. I hate tennis.
CAROLINE. Well, I want to play, David, and if I want
to play, then we shall play. I'll be waiting for you on the
court and you know I don't like to be kept waiting.
    DAVID. *(Beaten.)* Yes, Caroline. I'll be right there.
    CAROLINE. You look troubled, David. Is something
wrong?
    DAVID. No. Nothing.
    CAROLINE. That's good. I wouldn't want anything to
trouble you. My sweet, wonderful David. How lucky you
are to be you. Did you notice, I didn't say grateful again?
(SHE exits through the French doors.)
    SIMON. How do you stand it, David? How?

(DAVID sighs, and picks up his tennis racket.)

    STEFANIE. Poor weak, sad, David.

(DAVID looks at them for a beat.)

CAROLINE. (*O.S.*) David! I'm waiting!

(*DAVID looks off in Caroline's direction and then puts down the tennis racket and picks up the croquette mallet.*)

CHARLEY. She wants to play tennis today, David That's the croquette mallet you have.
DAVID. Is it now?
CAROLINE. (*O.S.*) David!
DAVID. (*Slaps the mallet in his hand.*) Coming, Caroline.

(*HE exits. The OTHERS rise to watch him in the distance.*)

MARIE. Do you think that maybe this time ...
SIMON. (*Turning away.*) Forget it. It'll never happen.

(*The OTHERS also turn away.*)

CHARLEY. You're probably right.

(*Suddenly offstage we hear a loud scream from CAROLINE. The FOUR on stage look at each other in bewilderment. DAVID enters. His mallet and his clothes are covered with blood. HE smiles at them and hands CHARLEY the mallet.*)

CHARLEY. Oh, my God. There's blood on it. This time there's blood.

(DAVID sits down and takes on a very pleased expression as the OTHERS look at him in amazement.)

DAVID. I hope everyone is satisfied now.

(The LIGHTS dim.)

CURTAIN
THE END

COSTUME PLOT

ACT I, SCENE 1
CAROLINE – Chic lounging gown
DAVID – Blue sweater jacket with collar, grey pants, shirt, tie
SIMON – Cardigan sweater, slacks, shirt, tie
STEFANIE – Black maid's dress, white apron
MARIE – Black maid's dress, white apron

ACT I, SCENE 2
CAROLINE – Sport slacks, blouse, flats
DAVID – Same as previous scene, no tie
SIMON – Suit jacket to pants in previous scene. shirt, tie.
STEFANIE – Short sleeve safari shirt, shorts, sandals
MARIE – Maid's outfit from previous scene

ACT I, SCENE 3
CAROLINE – chic afternoon dress
DAVID – Suit jacket to pants in previous scene, tie
STEFANIE – skirt, blouse
MARIE – Maid's outfit
CHARLIE – Blazer, shirt, slacks, loafers, no tie

ACT I, SCENE 4
CAROLINE – Same as Scene 3
DAVID – Same as Scene 3
SIMON – Sweater from scene 1
STEFANIE – Same as scene 3

MARIE – conservative black dress, pearls. Should be fashioned from maid's dress so that she can return to maid's costume later on in scene.
CHARLIE – Trench coat, scarf, jacket, shirt, tie

ACT II, SCENE 1
CAROLINE – Same as previous scene
DAVID – Same as previous scene
SIMON – Suit and tie
STEFANIE – Maid's outfit, 2nd entrance an evening coat, dressy earrings, shoes
MARIE – maid's outfit
CHARLIE – Same as previous scene,

ACT II, SCENE 2
CAROLINE – Same dress as previous scene, evening coat
DAVID – Same as previous scene
SIMON – Cardigan sweater, slacks, shirt, tie
STEFANIE – Same as last entrance in previous scene,
MARIE – Maid's outfit
CHARLIE – Same as last entrance in previous scene

ACT II, SCENE 3
CAROLINE – Same as previous scene, 2nd entrance tennis outfit
DAVID – Sweater jacket, slacks, no tie, later on add tennis sweater over shirt, 2nd entrance, bloody tennis sweater
SIMON – Same as previous scene
STEFANIE – Wholesome party dress
MARIE – Maid's outfit
CHARLIE – Leather bomber jacket, shirt, no tie. 2nd entrance, blazer from I,3.

PROPERTY PLOT

BASIC SET

Antique sofa
2 Queen Anne Chairs
2 small end tables
Long, narrow refectory type table, with drawer
Liquor cart, glasses, wine and whisky decanters
Small end table
Letter opener on refectory table
(NOTE: ALL KNIVES AND LETTER OPENERS USED
    AS WEAPONS ARE THE STAGE RETRACTABLE
    TYPE)
Appropriate books

PRE SET PROPS
I,3
Check book and pen in refectory table drawer
II,1
Tea cups, saucer
II,3
White tennis sweater – David
Tennis racket and croquet mallet in wicker basket.

CARRY ON PROPS
I,1
Small vial with liquid – David
I,2
Croquet mallet – Stefanie
Croquet mallet – Caroline

I,3
Attaché case – David
II,1
Tea tray, tea pot – Stefanie as maid
Man's wallet with woman's picture in plastic window –
  Charley
II,2
Ice bucket – Marie
Small medical bag with hypodermic needle
  inside – Simon
Tea tray, cups, saucers, tea pot – Marie
Knife – Charley
Tennis racket – Caroline

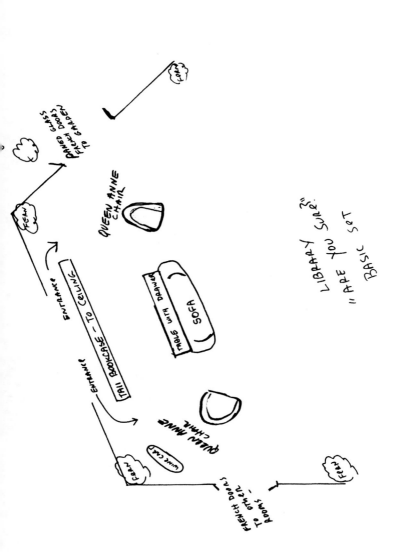